PENELOPE PERFECT

PRIVATE LIST FOR CAMP SUCCESS

Chrissie Perry

ALADDIN

NEW YORK LONDON TORONTO SYDNEY NEW DELHI

✦ ALADDIN

An imprint of Simon & Schuster Children's Publishing Division
1230 Avenue of the Americas, New York, New York 10020
First Aladdin paperback edition April 2017
Text copyright © 2015 by Chrissie Perry
Interior illustrations copyright © 2015 by Hardie Grant Egmont
Interior series design copyright © 2015 by Hardie Grant Egmont
Cover illustration copyright © 2017 by Marta Kissi
Published by arrangement with Hardie Grant Egmont
Originally published in Australia in 2015 by Hardie Grant Egmont
Also available in an Aladdin hardcover edition.
All rights reserved, including the right of reproduction in whole or in part in any form.
ALADDIN and related logo are registered trademarks of Simon & Schuster, Inc.
For information about special discounts for bulk purchases, please contact Simon & Schuster Special Sales at 1-866-506-1949 or business@simonandschuster.com.
The Simon & Schuster Speakers Bureau can bring authors to your live event. For more information or to book an event contact the Simon & Schuster Speakers Bureau at 1-866-248-3049 or visit our website at www.simonspeakers.com.
Cover designed by Laura Lyn DiSiena
The text of this book was set in Aldine 401 BT Std.
Manufactured in the United States of America 0317 OFF
10 9 8 7 6 5 4 3 2 1
Library of Congress Control Number 2016931522
ISBN 978-1-4814-6605-9 (hc)
ISBN 978-1-4814-6604-2 (pbk)
ISBN 978-1-4814-6606-6 (eBook)

PRIVATE LIST FOR CAMP SUCCESS

CHAPTER

Penelope Kingston knew that you were supposed to feel excited about going on a school camping trip. So Penelope was determined not to feel anxious. But sometimes she found it hard to tell the difference between feeling excited and feeling anxious. In fact, one moment she could feel excited, and then the very next moment, WHAM! She was worried and nervous all over again.

Penelope had been using some calming

techniques in the lead-up to the trip. She reminded herself that she had been on sleepovers before. Not as many as most other girls, but she had slept in Grandpa George's spare room lots of times. And she had gone to Tilly's slumber party back in first grade and been perfectly fine.

Plus, she had been to camp last year.

But thinking about last year's camp was *not* very helpful. In fact, it made Penelope's cheeks flush and her heart beat very fast. Unfortunately, last year's camp had not been perfect. Mr. Joseph had made them all climb a very steep and frightening hill.

PENELOPE HAD CRIED (ONLY TEARS, NOT SOBS).

She'd also had an outburst when she discovered that Joanna (the naughtiest girl in the class) had put lasagna in the bottom of Penelope's sleeping bag.

Penelope stopped that memory.

This time, things were going to be different. Completely different. After all, she was a whole year older. Even though (annoyingly) she had only grown an inch, and was still the smallest in her class, Penelope was *definitely* more mature on the inside.

AND (MORE IMPORTANTLY) THIS TIME, SHE WOULD HAVE HER VERY OWN BEST FRIEND TO SIT NEXT TO ON THE BUS AND SHARE A CABIN WITH.

Penelope was determined not to cry this year. And she was absolutely not going to have an outburst.

If she had an outburst at Camp Tribute, Penelope would *never* forgive herself.

Penelope unzipped the secret pocket of her duffel bag, which she had carefully packed. She pulled out her Private List. It was just a short list, and she knew it by heart. But she felt quite sure that having it in her bag, and knowing that she could sneak a look at it whenever she wanted, would be helpful.

LIST FOR CAMP SUCCESS
1. No outbursts
2. No crying
3. Win (at least one) prize
4. Try all activities ***

Penelope was quite sure about the first three rules. Since she first wrote the list (six days ago, when she'd packed her bag), she hadn't changed her mind about them one little bit.

She was less sure about the fourth rule, however. At last year's camp, when Penelope had (eventually) reached the top of that very steep hill, the fact that she had cried (only tears, not sobs) on the way up suddenly didn't seem so terrible. Penelope was just amazed she had actually done it. But this year's camp was famous for its activities. And they looked *way* more frightening than climbing up a (ridiculously) steep hill.

Penelope was just debating whether to erase "all" in rule four of her list (which would leave a funny space), or to simply put a question mark at the end, when her phone rang. It was only eight p.m., but Penelope had already showered and was ready for bed. She wanted to have a good precamp sleep.

Since her very own best friend had programmed the ringtone ("Boing," which was a very *jumpy* type of ringtone that Penelope would never have chosen herself), Penelope knew exactly who was on the phone.

A bolt of pleasure passed through her.

She put a (very elegant) question mark next to rule four on the list, erased "all," and wrote (in small letters, so it would fit nicely) "most" between "try" and "activities."

Then she answered the phone.

"Hi, Bob," she said to her very best friend.

"I am *seriously* pumped, Pen!" Bob squealed.

Penelope had never much liked having her name shortened. In fact, there were only two people who managed to do it without being annoying. Luckily, Bob (her very best friend) was one of them.

"It's tomorrow!" continued Bob. "*To-morrow!* Can you even believe it? We'll be going on the ropes course! And we'll be rock climbing! And the challenge swing! OMG. It's famous!"

Penelope felt a frown pulling her eyebrows together. There had been a lot of talk at school about the giant challenge swing. Every time it had been mentioned, Penelope had felt her tummy lurching.

She had a suspicion that some of the kids were only *pretending* to be excited about the swing. Although she was very good at deducing things, this kind of pretending was a great mystery to Penelope. For instance, she absolutely could not understand the way Tilly would walk out of every test complaining that she'd failed. Tilly had never failed a test—not one single time. Penelope was always able to judge (within a point or two) how she'd done on a test, and she was sure Tilly could do the same.

And some people were always pretending they hadn't put in any effort before an event. Her brother, Harry, did this all the time. Penelope had heard him tell his soccer teammates that he hadn't trained at all, when in fact Penelope had seen him kicking his soccer ball around every single day after school.

These things were very confusing. Even more confusing was that when Penelope (helpfully) told Tilly and Harry that they didn't need to pretend, they did not seem happy or relieved.

Embellishing was another thing Penelope did not understand. If everyone just stuck to

FACTS, life would be way less complicated.

For example, she was absolutely certain that kids were exaggerating when they talked about how high the challenge swing was.

Felix Unger (who had a habit of embellishing the truth) had been ridiculous enough to suggest it was almost one hundred and fifty feet high. That could absolutely, positively not be true!

AFTER ALL, PENELOPE'S HOUSE WAS TWO STORIES HIGH, AND THAT WAS ONLY TWENTY FEET.

Penelope closed her eyes and imagined herself rising into the sky on a giant swing. In fact, she imagined so hard that she felt quite giddy and almost forgot she was on the phone.

"Pen? Are you there?" Bob prompted.

"Yes," Penelope said, glad to be back down on earth. "And Bob, don't forget things like orienteering and outdoor cooking."

Penelope knew she would probably never be excellent at sports, or any kind of physical activity, but she was absolutely sure she would excel at many other things.

"It's going to be completely crazy-mad," Bob squealed.

Penelope giggled. Though she'd become used to the way Bob spoke, it still made her laugh. This, along with the way Bob wore her hair (extremely short with spikes at the top) and the way she insisted on being called Bob instead of Brittany O'Brien (which was her real name), was what made Bob a unique and fabulous very best friend.

"I wonder who'll end up in our cabin," Penelope said when she'd stopped giggling.

The students had each listed the three people they would most like to share a cabin with. Penelope and Bob had put each other first. (This had never happened to Penelope before, so she had checked Bob's list with her own eyes.)

Ms. Pike had already told the class that everyone got their first choice. But until they got to camp, they wouldn't know who else they were sharing a cabin with.

"I don't really mind who it is," Bob replied. "Sarah and Tilly would be good."

"Or maybe Eliza and Alison," Penelope continued.

"Even Joanna could be fun," Bob offered.

After last year's lasagna incident, Penelope wasn't sure about sharing a cabin with Joanna. Joanna was *absolutely* the naughtiest girl Penelope had ever met. She also had a terrible habit of sticking her tongue out in very unusual and disagreeable ways.

Still, she did have *some* good qualities. For instance, Joanna had been very apologetic after Penelope's outburst about the lasagna.

"Yep, even Joanna would be okay," Penelope replied.

The girls were silent for a moment.

"As long as it's not—"

"Don't!" Penelope said urgently. "Don't even say her name, or you'll jinx us."

"Okay," Bob said, "I won't say it starts with an *R*. And I won't say that the next letter is—"

"I have to go," Penelope interrupted. Even

though it may have *sounded* like a lie, and even though Penelope really did want to stop speaking about the person they really, really didn't want to share a cabin with, it was actually true that Penelope needed to go.

Because just then there was a very loud bang on Penelope's bedroom wall that needed immediate investigation.

CHAPTER

2

Although Penelope was usually pretty calm and sensible, sometimes (she had to admit) she could be really bossy and cranky. It was like there were two different Penelopes living inside her. It was the angry, frustrated Penelope who (sometimes) had outbursts. Outbursts were terribly exhausting and embarrassing, so she had been practicing how NOT to have one. She was *determined* to stick to the number one rule on her list.

Instead, she started to type "Camp Tribute" into the search engine on her iPhone. She'd looked at the camp's website before, of course, but suddenly it seemed necessary to confirm the exact height of the challenge swing. She was sure she'd seen the word "optional" somewhere.

If she wasn't *required* to go on the challenge swing, she could put her energy into being excellent at some other activity. (Penelope was very glad she'd changed her list to read "try *most* activities.") She thought she might be quite good at orienteering. Orienteering was about being careful and thorough, and Penelope was definitely careful and thorough.

She had typed the first six letters into the search engine when there was another bang on the wall. This time it was followed by a burst of music.

"We will, we will rock you!"

Penelope put down her iPhone and crossed her arms. Harry had a basketball hoop in his bedroom, and even though the ball was soft, it still made a loud banging sound when it hit the wall. Even worse, the ball was most likely covered with something disgusting. There was always a range of disgusting things to choose from on Harry's floor. The last time she'd looked under his bed, Penelope had counted three smelly socks, a hairy orange, and two ancient, half-eaten pieces of Hawaiian pizza.

Whenever the ball hit the wall, she imagined it releasing a fungus colony that would multiply and spread into her own (neat and clean) bedroom.

Penelope opened her middle drawer and sprayed some antibacterial spray around the room, just in case. Then she went back to her phone. She had only managed to type in "Camp Trib" when another bang interrupted her. PENELOPE LOOKED IN THE MIRROR AND SAW THAT HER NOSTRILS WERE FLARED. She concentrated on unflaring them. She was still determined not to react (even though it *was* the night before camp, and Harry really should have more consideration).

The best thing was to stay calm and definitely not have an outburst. In fact, this was Very Good practice. Penelope walked casually toward Harry's room.

Her mom was standing in the doorway, cheering Harry on. Penelope was quite sure that most mothers would not do that.

"You need to aim a bit to your right, Haz," she was saying.

Penelope paused in the hallway and watched over her mom's shoulder as Harry jumped on his bed and threw the ball. Though she couldn't see the hoop, she could tell Harry had got it in. Her mom's face lit up. She was on her second air punch when she noticed Penelope standing there.

"Oh hello, Poss," she said. She hesitated midpunch, as though she wasn't entirely sure whether to continue.

For some reason, that made Penelope a little bit sad. Even though her mom and Harry were quite different from her, and sometimes the things they liked seemed silly to Penelope, she didn't want to ruin their fun.

"So," said her mom, "are you all ready? It's so exciting. Harry loved Camp Tribute." She turned to Harry. "Didn't you, Haz? Any advice for your little sister?"

Harry's bed squeaked as he jumped onto the floor. His Batman pajama pants had big holes in the knees, and he was wearing his Space Invaders T-shirt, which was much too small. The combination was quite difficult for Penelope to look at.

"Camp Tribute is awesome," Harry said. "You'll love it. You should try to do all the activities."

Penelope did not roll her eyes.

"I'm planning to throw myself into outdoor cooking, and I think I might be quite good at orienteering," she said.

Harry looked a bit confused, as though he had never heard of those activities. Penelope supposed that was because camp was such a long time ago for Harry. He probably couldn't remember much about it at all.

"Just make sure you go on the challenge swing," Harry said. "It's sick! Do you know it's over sixty feet high?"

"I'm quite sure the challenge swing is *optional*," Penelope said a little snappily.

It was a shock to hear that the swing was more than THREE TIMES THE HEIGHT of their house. It was also a shock that Harry remembered the exact height. He wasn't the type of person who usually paid attention to detail.

A series of images ran quickly through Penelope's brain.

THE FIRST IMAGE WAS OF BOB (HER VERY OWN BEST FRIEND) SWINGING HIGH IN THE AIR AND THEN COMING DOWN, GRINNING MADLY, TO A CROWD OF KIDS WHO WERE CHEERING AND CLAPPING.

SECOND WAS AN IMAGE OF OSCAR FINLEY (WHO WAS USUALLY NOT THAT GOOD AT SPORTS) FLYING THROUGH THE AIR AND RECEIVING BACK-PATS AND HOOTS FROM THE OTHER KIDS.

FINALLY, PENELOPE SAW AN IMAGE OF HERSELF, BEING PUSHED AND PRODDED AND FORCED TO GO ON THE SWING.

Even though it was just an image, and not real, suddenly the feelings Penelope had been trying to squash down by *not reacting* rushed past the calm and nice part of her. Penelope felt doomed to have an outburst at camp in front of everyone, no matter how hard she tried not to.

"Hey, remember not to hold your breath, Penelope," Harry said.

Sometimes Penelope would hold her breath without even realizing it. This was not a good thing to do, because (as the girl whose name began with *R* had pointed out) it made her red in the face, and it made her veins pop out.

"There are loads of nerdy activities, too," Harry said, after Penelope started breathing again. "You'll be fine."

"Of course you will, Poss," her mom joined in. "I know you'll have a great time."

Even though Penelope was not keen on

Harry describing the kind of activities Penelope liked as "nerdy," and even though her mother couldn't *really* know that Penelope would have a great time, Penelope felt a little better.

But worrying a bit less about camp just opened up some room for worries about her mom and Harry.

Without Penelope there to organize things, the two of them could definitely run into problems.

"The question is, will you two be okay?" she asked.

Although she was quite serious, her mom and Harry were smiling. Penelope sighed. Honestly, Harry and her mom didn't understand how *important* she was when it came to keeping their house organized.

"Mom, you'll need to buy healthy food," Penelope reminded her. There was a good chance that Harry and her mom would eat junk food the whole time she was gone if Penelope wasn't strict with them.

"I will shop as though you're right there with me," her mom promised. Penelope was pleased to see her mom had her hand on her heart as she spoke, which meant it was a *core promise*. A core promise was one you couldn't break (no matter what).

Penelope knew a lot about core promises because her dad was a politician, and politicians made core promises quite a lot.

"Harry, what are the five major groups in the food pyramid?" she quizzed.

Now that she had a core promise to reassure her, Penelope felt quite playful. They'd played this game a million times, but there was something about the silly way Harry always answered that Penelope loved.

"UM, LET'S SEE. FIRST IT'S PIZZA, THEN CHIPS, THEN CHOCOLATE. NO, WAIT, IT'S CHIPS, THEN SODA, THEN IT'S—"

"You're impossible, Harry!" Penelope interrupted, rolling her eyes.

But it was quite big-brotherly and night-before-camp-ish when Harry ruffled her hair. Penelope rather liked it—even though her hair had been neatly brushed, and would have to be brushed again now.

When Penelope got back to her room, there was a message from Grandpa George on her iPhone:

> Enjoy the ride. Remember, the journey is just as important as the destination. Miss you already. G x

Penelope considered the message. The bus trip to Camp Tribute was expected to take two hours and thirty-five minutes. So the bus ride could not possibly be as important as the destination. She'd be at camp for two whole nights (or approximately forty-eight hours).

Penelope adored getting messages from Grandpa George, but sometimes they didn't make absolute sense.

She tucked her iPhone under her pillow, which felt a little bit like having Grandpa close by. Then she pulled blue teddy close to her chest, thinking he might need a hug before she went away for approximately forty-eight hours, and fell asleep.

CHAPTER

3

Before leaving the next morning, Penelope grabbed her phone and snapped some last-minute pictures of herself and her luggage.

On the way to school, she added some pictures of the footpath and the sky and labeled them EIGHT A.M. She sent them to her dad, along with a link to the Camp Tribute website.

Each week, Penelope would send her dad a photo of her school timetable so he would know exactly what she was doing at any time.

But since Penelope had absolutely no idea of the camp timetable, he would just have to make do with general information about the camp.

Then she took a selfie of her blowing a kiss to her half sister, Sienna.

"Good-bye, iPhone," she said, reluctantly handing it to her mom, who had come to help Penelope carry all her camp gear, and to say good-bye.

"Don't worry, Poss," said her mom. "I'll put it in your special box with the lock and key."

Penelope had a wobbly feeling as she gave up her phone for forty-eight hours. There was another strange feeling when her mom hugged her. It was as though the hug was squishing her excitement and her nerves together in quite a messy way. Penelope was worried she was going to break rule number two on her Private List—before they even got on the bus!

Luckily, right at that moment, Penelope saw over her mom's shoulder that Oscar Finley needed immediate rescuing.

A few kids were gathered around Oscar. He had his arm outstretched and was showing something to the others. Even without knowing *exactly* what Oscar was showing them, Penelope could make an educated guess: some kind of bug or insect. Oscar was a great lover of nature. He knew lots of different types of birds and beetles. He even loved spiders (which Penelope definitely didn't agree with). He knew many interesting facts about them.

The problem, as Penelope saw it, was that Oscar was totally distracted by whatever he was showing the others. So distracted, in fact, that he did not notice the bus driver putting both of his bags—his luggage *and* his backpack—into the underneath compartment of the bus (which would soon be locked up). They had all been told to put their lunches and water bottles in their backpacks and to bring them on the bus.

Penelope hugged her mom tight. It was a Very Nice Hug and she would have liked it to go on for longer, but she couldn't stand the thought of Oscar Finley having to go without lunch or even a drink. She felt a pang as she said good-bye to her mom and pulled away.

Penelope went over to explain the situation to the bus driver, then she took Oscar's backpack over to him.

"Look, Penny," Oscar said before she could say anything. He showed her the bug on his hand.

(Penelope had completely given up trying to get Oscar Finley to use her proper name. The strange thing was, she had actually started *liking* it when he called her Penny.)

"It's a praying mantis. It gets its name from the way it clasps its forelegs together, as though it's praying. Would you like to hold it?"

Penelope shook her head. The praying mantis was like a very tall, leggy grasshopper. It was quite nice to *look* at, but that was definitely enough for her.

Penelope glanced over at the bus. The driver had just finished packing all the bags and was closing the door to the compartment. Oscar still hadn't realized his backpack was missing.

"The praying mantis is the only insect that can swivel its head a full one-eighty degrees," Oscar continued, as the other kids began to line up for the bus. Penelope felt a fluttering feeling in her tummy as she saw Bob (her very best friend) standing near the front of the line. The fluttering got worse when she saw that the line was moving.

"Can you believe that, Penny? Isn't it awesome?"

"It's a very interesting fact, Oscar," Penelope said. "But we need to get going. Here's your backpack."

Penelope handed the backpack to Oscar and walked very quickly over to the line. When she looked back, she saw that Oscar was carefully putting the praying mantis in a tree, as if he had all the time in the world.

Finally, much to Penelope's relief, he joined the very end of the line.

Oscar pointed to his backpack, and then he put his hands together. He moved them up to his forehead like a praying mantis.

"Thanks, Penny," he said. "You're the best."

In other circumstances, Oscar Finley mimicking a praying mantis would have made Penelope giggle. Just then, though, Penelope was too distracted by her fluttery feeling about not being next to Bob in the line.

She should have joined Bob. Or asked her to wait. Or Penelope should have got to the front of the line herself, when she'd first arrived at school. Now it was too late!

When she got to the bottom step, Penelope stood on her tiptoes and craned her neck, trying to see into the bus. But Bob seemed to have disappeared.

PENELOPE HAD A SUDDEN, HORRIBLE IMAGE OF HER VERY BEST FRIEND SQUASHED INTO THE BACK ROW OF THE BUS, WITH ABSOLUTELY NO SPACE LEFT FOR PENELOPE.

Then, as if that weren't bad enough, she imagined a certain person whose name began with *R* sitting (in a very determined way) right next to Bob. Now that Penelope (finally) had her very own best friend, it would be heartbreaking if she couldn't sit with her!

By now Penelope had reached the top of the stairs. She *still* couldn't see Bob. She was a third of the way down the aisle when she saw two empty seats.

As she reached the seats, Penelope saw that they were not actually empty. There was a hand planted on one seat. Someone was on the floor, rummaging through their backpack. There was no mistaking the head. The crest was sticking right up.

"Nope. That seat's for Penelope," Bob said, not looking up.

The fluttery feeling in Penelope's tummy

completely disappeared. **There was nothing quite like the feeling of having your very own best friend save you a seat on the bus.**

As they traveled along the freeway, Joanna tried to start everyone singing a rude song.

"We wanna, we wanna, we wanna wee.

If you don't stop for us, we'll do it on the bus."

Quite a few kids joined in. Joanna might be the naughtiest girl in Penelope's class, but she also had a very lovely singing voice. Soon after that song fizzled, someone else started up with some songs from *The Sound of Music*.

Penelope was tempted to block her ears so she didn't have to listen to Tommy Stratton singing. He did *not* have a lovely singing voice. If Penelope's voice were anywhere near as terrible as his, she would never sing a single note in public. But Tommy Stratton didn't seem bothered. He was VERY enthusiastic.

After the fifth round of "Do-Re-Mi," one of the teachers offered to put on a DVD.

"Yeah," someone groaned, "spare us from the torture of Tommy Tone-deaf."

Penelope very much hoped that Tommy hadn't heard.

She suspected she knew who had made that comment. She looked behind her. Directly behind her, she saw Oscar. Penelope had never (not even once) witnessed Oscar being mean. Oscar wouldn't harm a fly. (Literally.) But sitting behind Oscar, staring out the window and whistling as though it *definitely* weren't her, was the girl whose name began with *R*.

Rita Azul.

Penelope did not hate one single person

in the whole world. But she would be happy never to see Rita Azul again. Rita had always been a little bit mean (most likely since birth). But she seemed to be getting better at it all the time. Penelope supposed that Rita's meanness was a sort of skill that she had practiced and improved on. Kind of like Joanna's tongue poking, but nastier.

"That was definitely *her*," Bob said, nudging Penelope. "She's trying too hard not to look suspicious."

Penelope nodded. She and Bob were very different from each other in lots of ways. But it was very satisfying to have a best friend who was as good as her at piecing clues together.

The DVD finished loading and *Finding Nemo* came on. Penelope and Bob rested their heads together. It seemed to Penelope that the same thought was jumping from her head to

Bob's and then right back again. It was like they were swapping brain waves.

We should stay away from Rita Azul at camp.

The funny thing about having a new best friend is that you are still learning things about them. A New Thing Penelope learned about Bob was that traveling on the bus put Bob to sleep. And when Bob was asleep, there wasn't much that would wake her up.

Joanna and Tommy singing "Ninety-Nine Bottles of Beer" didn't rouse her.

Bob's head bumping (quite hard) against the window didn't even do it.

After the third bump, though, Penelope gently moved Bob's head to rest on her shoulder. Although she had to sit very still to keep it there, Penelope didn't mind. She figured this was the sort of thing you were supposed to do for your very best friend. Even if it did make the journey a tiny bit boring, and meant that enjoying the ride (as Grandpa had encouraged) was not really possible.

When the bus finally pulled into Camp Tribute, Bob woke with a start.

"Eeew, dribble on Penelope's shoulder much, Bob?" Rita said.

The way Rita swiveled her head as she walked past them reminded Penelope of Oscar's praying mantis. Except that the praying mantis was probably nicer. Tilly and Sarah giggled as they followed Rita.

Penelope felt her nostrils flaring. There was, in fact, a small wet patch on her shoulder. She would change T-shirts as soon as she possibly could. But it wasn't nice for Rita to draw attention to Bob's dribble. If it had been *Penelope*'s dribble on someone's T-shirt, she would have been horrified. But Bob didn't seem to care (really and truly, not in a pretending way).

"Oh. My. God. This place looks awesome!" Bob said, jumping out of her seat. Penelope and Bob grabbed their packs and followed everyone else off the bus.

There were trees everywhere. Penelope could see several cabins tucked away, and a pathway connecting them. In front of the bus, just a few feet away, was a very large hall. The ocean glistened in the distance.

Penelope felt her heartbeat quicken. Although she secretly thought the word "awesome" was overused, she had to agree with Bob.

CAMP TRIBUTE LOOKED AWESOME.

CHAPTER

Penelope sat cross-legged, her Camp Tribute booklet in front of her. She listened intently as a camp leader, Rachel, addressed them in the main hall. "You will take from this camp whatever you put into it," she said.

Rachel looked very fit and outdoorsy. She definitely didn't seem like the sort of camp leader who would be at all worried about a ridiculously high swing.

"But it's also about challenging yourself,"

continued Rachel. "It's about developing your self-esteem, and supporting others to do the same. I really encourage you all to—"

"Can you tell us about the challenge swing?" Joanna called out.

Although it was most certainly not polite to interrupt a camp leader, Rachel didn't seem to mind.

"Well, the challenge swing is over sixty feet high," Rachel began.

This was probably one of the first times in history that Penelope's brother had been right about that kind of detail. Penelope urged her tummy to stay calm.

"It's always our most popular activity," Rachel continued, "so it's likely you'll each get only one turn. But there are many other activities, too. There's a ropes course, and a rock-climbing wall. . . ."

Just then, Bob pinched Penelope's thigh. For a second, Penelope felt angry. But when she looked around, Bob was grinning. Perhaps pinching her thigh was a good, sharing-the-moment type of thing to do, rather than an annoying, distracting one? Perhaps it was something that very best friends did in such situations.

"There are also different *kinds* of challenges," Rachel was saying when Penelope managed to zone back in properly. "For instance, the competition for the best cabin is also very popular with students. I suspect it's largely because of this."

Rachel fished something out of a canvas bag behind her and held it up for everyone to see.

Penelope pinched Bob (quite hard) on the thigh. Because this was a moment she definitely wanted to share.

Penelope felt a little bit swoony looking at that medal.

She glanced over at Eliza Chung. Eliza was Class Captain. Penelope had really wanted to be Class Captain, but she was pretty sure only two people had voted for her: Oscar and Penelope herself. (This was before Bob came to their school, of course.)

Being Class Captain meant Eliza had a lovely badge she got to wear to school *every day*. Although Penelope had a whole wall of award certificates (and even more tucked away in her special box with a lock and key), she'd *never* owned a badge like Eliza's or a shiny medal like this.

But a best cabin competition was totally and completely suited to Penelope's talents. It was a better fit than outdoor cooking or even orienteering.

Penelope's mind immediately surged with excellent best cabin-ish plans. Rachel hadn't said anything about appointing a cabin leader, but it was clear to Penelope that her group would have a huge advantage if she volunteered for the role.

That way, while other teams were messing around discussing what to do, Penelope's group could just follow her instructions. They'd be way ahead.

She could already imagine how the medal would look on several of her (and Bob's) favorite outfits.

Most of the girls Penelope knew would probably think of it as a chore, since it would involve a lot of organizing. But Penelope knew that leading her cabin to victory would *definitely* not be a chore. In fact, she was super ready to find out who was in their cabin so they could get started straightaway.

"So, here are the cabin groups," Rachel said, after spending a lot of time talking about far less important things.

Penelope waited and waited and waited as Rachel read out the groups. It was *extremely* good to know that Bob was going to be in her cabin, but it was still worrying to *not know* who else would be with them. She looked across the hall. Oscar smiled and gave Penelope a big wave. She responded with a smaller one, keeping her hand by her side so no one else could see. Some of the kids could get very silly about things like boys and girls waving to each other.

When Oscar's group was read out, Penelope couldn't help glancing over to see if he was happy. Personally, she couldn't think of *any* other boys she would want to share a cabin with, but she was glad to see Oscar looked pleased. She was going to keep looking, and sneak him a smile when he glanced her way again. But then he started picking at a scab on his knee, and she decided against it. Even Very Nice Boys like Oscar Finley could be exceptionally gross.

As each group was called out, a camp leader took them off to their cabin. It was hard having to wait, but Penelope sat up straight and tried not to fidget. When Joanna went off to her cabin with Eliza, Alison, and Sarah, Penelope couldn't help feeling concerned about her chances of winning the best cabin medal.

Penelope knew that Joanna couldn't help being naughty, most of the time at least, so she wasn't really a threat. But Eliza Chung (Class Captain) and Alison Cromwell (who had collected twenty-five awards at school and was still coming second to Penelope's forty-one awards) were quite focused. Penelope guessed that they would be her strongest competition for best cabin.

But there were still sixteen kids and four cabins left. Penelope assumed that her group would be called last (mainly to help control her feelings of impatience).

So when Rachel read out, "Cabin seven! Penelope Kingston," Penelope got quite a shock.

Bob pinching her again did not help.

"Brittany O'Brien," Rachel continued.

Bob's hand (the one that was not pinching

Penelope) shot up in the air. Penelope already knew what Bob was going to say.

"I don't go by that name, Rachel. Not ever. Just call me Bob," she said.

Penelope waited as Rachel found a pen and made a note. It seemed to take a long time. Penelope estimated about eleven seconds, but if she had her iPhone she would have been able to measure exactly how long they waited.

Finally, Rachel continued. "Tilly Fraser and Rita Azul."

The cabin was quite bare and plain, with four bunk beds, a wardrobe with drawers at the bottom, and a small bathroom down the end. Someone had put cardboard name tags into the little metal frames at the end of each bed.

Penelope was pleased to see her name on a bottom bunk, with Bob's on top. Top bunks were terribly overrated (and a little hazardous) as far as Penelope was concerned.

Penelope put down her duffel bag on her allocated bed.

"The weird thing is," Rita said, glancing around the cabin as Bob crossed out BRITTANY on her name tag and wrote BOB instead, and Tilly climbed up to her top bunk, "seven is my lucky number."

Penelope tilted her head. "Really?" she said. "It's mine, too."

Rita smiled. It was actually quite a nice smile and not mean at all.

"You know, I think we should really, really try to win the best cabin competition," Rita continued. She dropped her voice to a whisper. "But

I think we need a secret weapon. We should have a leader. Someone who knows how to get everything organized."

Penelope could hardly believe her ears. There was no doubt Rita was talking about her. Out of all the kids in her class, Penelope was the only one, for example, who put the books in her locker in alphabetical order. Quite often, students from other grades even asked to see her locker. That was definitely proof of her of being super organized! In fact, she had a *reputation* for it!

And having Rita supporting her would be great, because Rita was a Very Determined Person.

Penelope was just about to start outlining her plans when Tilly stuck her head (rather dangerously) over the edge of her bunk.

"Guys," she squealed. "Check it out! I got

a welcome postcard from the girl who slept in this bunk before me!"

"Me, too," said Bob. "Don't you think that's a bit spooky? Kind of like getting a postcard from a ghost. Woooo!"

Penelope would have preferred to continue discussing the best cabin competition. Getting postcards from the people who'd stayed there before them was nothing like getting a postcard from a ghost (since, as far as they knew, no one who'd stayed here had actually died).

She assumed her postcard would be quite dull—something that the girl before her had been forced to write before she went home. But since everyone else was reading their postcards, Penelope quickly snuck into the bathroom and changed into a fresh, dribble-free T-shirt. Then she checked her bed for a postcard.

Dear (insert name),

POST CARD

Stamp

You may be feeling homesick or you may be worried about doing some of the activities at Camp Tribute. Remember, you can always go and hang out with the turtles or the guinea pigs.

But you shouldn't worry too much—all you have to do is try.

My advice is to give everything a try, and to let your hair down and enjoy your time here. Also, the BEST CABIN COMPETITION is really tough, so try everything you can think of to help you win.

From yours truly,
the Awesome and Talented
Poppy Katz, Cabin seven

Penelope read the postcard three times. Even though it definitely wasn't from a ghost, there *was* something spooky about it (in a good way). For starters, the writer shared Penelope's initials: Poppy Katz/Penelope Kingston. And even though the advice to try *everything* was a little bit annoying, it wasn't half as annoying as the other girls' postcards, which were all about the challenge swing—complete with drawings. And Poppy's advice about the best cabin competition was actually quite useful. Penelope quickly checked the notes in the Camp Tribute booklet.

WAYS TO GET BONUS POINTS

- Arrange your boots and shoes outside in a creative way, e.g., smiley face.
- Decorate your cabin with posters and drawings from the library or with your own artwork.
- Make sure the last person out of the cabin checks that *all lights are off*.

Penelope felt particularly excited about the middle point. She was excellent at art. She could already imagine the walls of cabin seven decorated with her drawings of local plants and animals. She tried to get Bob and Tilly's attention, but they were being a bit silly, putting their sleeping bags over their heads (in the top bunks!) and pretending to be ghosts.

She was about to announce her excellent idea out loud—loud enough be heard through sleeping bags—when there came a knock at the door. A camp leader (RAMON, his name badge said) opened the door. He took off his hat and bowed.

"Tour time, cabin seven," he said.

Rita peered over Penelope's shoulder. "Those are really good tips," she whispered as Bob and Tilly jumped down from their bunks. "We need to pay attention to them."

Even though Penelope didn't like people reading over her shoulder, she decided to let it go. Rita was right. And she was being so agreeable.

Perhaps sharing a cabin with Rita Azul wouldn't be such a bad thing after all.

CHAPTER

Three other cabins joined cabin seven for the tour of Camp Tribute. Oscar's cabin was there, plus another boys' cabin, and cabin six (with Joanna, Eliza, Alison, and Sarah).

Penelope was a little surprised to see Joanna walking right next to Alex Gabriel, chatting away happily. It was kind of a rule that boys and girls stayed pretty separate outside of class.

Penelope actually chatted with Oscar quite

a bit, like when they were working on a charity booth together, or when they were looking at Oscar's weird bugs. But she always thought that was because Oscar was just that sort of boy. It was most unusual to see a girl like Joanna and a boy like Alex spending so much time together.

The group stopped (with Joanna and Alex leaning into each other in quite a strange way) as Ramon pointed out the bike ed course.

The next stop was the rock-climbing wall. Penelope had done a bit of rock climbing with Harry and her dad, when he was in town over the holidays. Her dad had switched off his cell phone completely and absolutely (not even on vibrate) and stayed with them for a whole hour. Penelope had trusted her brain to help her feet find the right spot, and it had worked. She still remembered that day vividly.

Her dad had said that she and Harry were "mountain goats" (which was apparently a compliment if you were rock climbing). And afterward, he had taken them out for Chinese food, just the three of them—no stepmother or Sienna.

Although it was a type of sport, Penelope quite liked rock climbing.

The next stop was a lovely art room. As the art teacher showed them around, Penelope took note of the materials she could use for the pictures she was planning to draw, which would be vital to her group winning the best cabin competition.

Then they looked at the archery area, and the ropes course. Unfortunately, the ropes course wasn't an optional activity (Penelope had asked). Still, it didn't look ridiculously hard. Penelope thought she would cope.

When they came to the challenge swing, however, Penelope had to remind herself to breathe.

IT LOOKED A BIT LIKE A REGULAR PLAYGROUND SWING, EXCEPT THAT IT WAS MORE THAN THREE TIMES THE HEIGHT OF HER HOUSE.

"The challenge swing is an optional activity," Ramon said. "But you *do* have to sit in the harness and get the feel of it. The people on the ground pull on the rope, which causes the harness to rise. When you've gone as high as you want, you release yourself by tugging on this green handle."

Penelope shut her eyes. Now the swing was right in front of her, she could practically *feel* herself rising up into the sky. In fact, she could imagine it so clearly she felt more giddy than she'd ever felt before. But she could *absolutely not* imagine pulling that green handle, knowing that she would instantly *plummet to the ground*.

"I'm going all the way to the top and I'm going to do tricks," said Alex loudly. "I'm going to fly like Superman!"

Penelope felt her eyebrows arching. For some reason that seemed to have little to do with the challenge swing *or* Superman, Alex then got Joanna in a headlock. As far as Penelope was concerned, he was acting very strangely. Perhaps the idea of *plummeting to the ground* had made him a little crazy?

"Me, too," Rita called out. "I'm going all the way to the top, and I'm going to sing when I'm up there. Really, really loudly!"

Penelope's nose twitched as Rita started singing really, really loudly.

"*This stuff is bananas,*" she sang at the top of her voice. "*B-A-N-A-N-A-S.*"

Tilly and Sarah joined in the song, just like they often did at school. It made Penelope feel tense in her neck and shoulders.

There was something weird—and maybe a

bit mean—about the way Rita sang that song. For instance, one time Mr. Cattapan, the art teacher, had put Penelope's painting up in the display cabinet outside the art room. Rita had stood right in front of it and sung that song, as though she didn't care at all. But earlier, Penelope had overheard Rita begging Mr. Cattapan to pick her painting for the display cabinet.

In fact, if Penelope didn't know better, she might think Rita was just pretending to be pumped about the challenge swing.

Penelope shook her head, trying to shake off these difficult thoughts. She would just have to be tolerant. After all, she and Rita were finally starting to get along.

Unfortunately, standing there listening to the silly song, and to the other kids (who might or might not have been pretending to be excited—she couldn't tell) was making Penelope feel not-very-tolerant. So she was glad when Ramon started to move on.

It was quite calming to listen to Ramon point out the different types of trees and flowers and shrubs around the camp. Penelope felt a lot better when Oscar asked for scientific names and repeated the spellings out loud so he would remember them. Thank goodness she wasn't the only one focused on something other than that silly swing. She was already thinking about drawing the coastal tea tree. To do it properly would take a long time, but it would be worth it when they won the best cabin competition.

The next stop was the orienteering cabin. Ramon tried to sound spooky as he pointed to a sign above the cabin. COFFIN CURVES. "If you follow the instructions, all you ghouls should end up here, right where you started," he said in a wobbly voice that sounded more funny than frightening. "On the way, you will have to pass through Madness Mountain, Blood River, and many more, and check them off your list." Lots of kids pretended to be afraid, but there was a *lot* of giggling going on. After that, Ramon handed them over to another camp leader, Kayla.

Kayla led the group through a marine center, where they saw the turtles (which were quite dignified and lovely) that Poppy had written about in her postcard. Penelope would have liked to spend more time with the turtles, but Kayla was already leading them into the barn next door.

On the far side of the barn there were three enclosures with straw spread out on the floor and several homemade cardboard shelters with little arched doorways. Penelope counted a total of twenty-six guinea pigs (though some may have been hiding).

Most of the kids had been quiet during the tour of the marine center, but something about the guinea pigs seemed to change the atmosphere.

"OMG!" Joanna squealed. "Can we hold them?"

Penelope took a few steps backward. She didn't mind looking at the guinea pigs, but she was in even less of a hurry to hold one than she had been to hold Oscar's praying mantis. Penelope was pretty sure the guinea pigs weren't toilet-trained. What if one decided to poo just when she was holding it?

Luckily, holding the guinea pigs was optional.

"Why don't you get into pairs and choose a

guinea pig," Kayla suggested. "There are grooming brushes hung up on the wall, or you can feed them grass from the courtyard."

Since Penelope didn't want to actually pick up a guinea pig, she decided to take a grooming brush from a hook on the wall. She hoped that Bob would hold a guinea pig on her lap. That way, Penelope might get to brush its fur. She was (quite) sure she would be okay with that. Penelope was just about to sit on a haystack next to Bob when Tilly got there first.

Penelope held her breath. Bob was her very own best friend, and this wasn't really fair. She thought about asking Tilly to move, but it was hard to think of how to do that without sounding bossy. Instead, she took three deep breaths and sat next to Alison Cromwell.

"This little guy is called Alfie," Alison said. Alison was very good at handling her guinea pig, even though Alfie was definitely not little. In fact, he was so enormous he could barely fit on her lap.

Penelope glanced over at Bob, who was now stroking a black-and-white guinea pig while Tilly fed it some grass. As Penelope reached over to brush Alfie, she made a mental note to ask Bob whether she'd ever had any pets. She also reminded herself to let Bob know that she'd had a fish called Harold Holt until he (tragically) floated to the top of the tank for the last time a year ago. It seemed like the sort of thing she and Bob should know about each other given they were (as Tilly knew) very best friends.

Kayla was busy helping Sarah rescue her guinea pig (which had taken off and was now hiding inside one of the boxes) when Alex stood up and put his guinea pig up under his

T-shirt. He rolled it up so that a bit of his stomach showed, then walked over to Joanna and bumped her.

"Ta-dah!" he said, as though he had performed a magic trick (which was quite silly, since the lump in his T-shirt was so obviously guinea-pig shaped).

Even though Penelope did not know much about guinea pigs, she suspected they did not like being rolled up in T-shirts or being bumped into people. But she did not have to say a single word because Rita was very, very quick.

"STOP. GUINEA PIGS DO NOT LIKE THAT, ALEX!" she said firmly. She unrolled his T-shirt and confiscated the animal, then held the guinea pig to her chest protectively.

"You are absolutely right," Kayla said to Rita as she came back into the barn. She addressed everyone. "Be very gentle with the guinea pigs, please. They are not toys. If you treat them well, you'll find that they can make very lovely pets."

Rita gave Alex an I-told-you-so look. Penelope knew that look very well, but this time, she agreed with Rita.

"Just one thing," Kayla said to Rita. "I think you'll find that Florence is upside down."

Rita grimaced with embarrassment but Kayla just smiled. "Don't worry. Florence gets that quite a lot. Having such long fur makes it difficult to tell her head from her bottom!"

Everyone laughed as Rita put Florence, who did look a little jittery, the right way up.

Penelope watched, entranced by the way Rita calmed Florence down. She stroked the animal rhythmically again and again, and after a while, Florence nuzzled into Rita's chest.

Watching Rita pat Florence almost made Penelope feel like petting a guinea pig herself. In fact, Rita's patience and attention made Penelope start to think that perhaps Rita could help to fill in the detail on Penelope's drawings. The veins on the leaves could be very tricky and time-consuming.

As cabin leader, Penelope was definitely open to finding the best use for Rita's talents.

"You were very good with the guinea pigs, Rita," Penelope said graciously when they got back to their cabin. She said it in front of Bob and Tilly so Rita would feel extra special.

"Well, *you* weren't. You didn't even hold one," Rita said. "You really need to try new things, Penelope, or you'll never grow and develop. I hope you'll have the guts to go on the challenge swing."

Bob and Tilly were *still* right there, listening, which made Rita's comment even meaner. Penelope felt a sudden urge to sing: *This stuff is bananas. B-A-N-A-N-A-S.*

But to keep the peace as cabin leader, Penelope did not sing the song. Maybe all her practice had worked. She hadn't made a fuss when Tilly sat next to Bob in the barn, and now she let Rita's mean comment go without reacting at all.

Bike ed was next, then after dinner they had to choose between art and outdoor cooking. Penelope knew what she'd be doing. It was essential to get started on the drawings tonight (as well as Penelope's plans for keeping their cabin very tidy and organized).

Penelope took a deep breath, ready to say

some very inspirational things. But Rita had already started talking.

"Cabin seven is totally going to win best cabin," she said in her big, enthusiastic voice. "And I'm going to lead the way."

CHAPTER

Even though she knew dragons were fictional characters and had never, not even in the very olden days, been real . . .

PENELOPE COULD ABSOLUTELY IMAGINE FLAMES SHOOTING FROM HER NOSE RIGHT AT THAT MOMENT.

Luckily, she was able to benefit from all her practice at *not reacting*. She glanced at her duffel bag and thought of the list she had tucked away in the secret pocket.

She knew that no matter how upset she might feel, and no matter what Rita said, number one on the checklist was very clear:

No outbursts

When Penelope spoke, her voice was a little wobbly and her top and bottom teeth seemed to be stuck together. But she was not yelling, and the veins in her temples still felt flat.

"Actually, Rita," she said, as calmly as she could, "I think I should be the leader. I've got a lot of excellent ideas."

"Well," said Rita, "let's all think about this."

Penelope noticed that Bob and Tilly were both looking down, as though they didn't want to be there.

"Who is older, you or me?" Rita demanded.

Rita was the oldest girl in the whole class. Everyone knew that.

"You are," Penelope said. "But that's not—"

"And who is taller, you or me?" Rita interrupted rudely.

Penelope glowered. Just recently, they'd had to line up in order of size for the school photo. As the shortest girl in their class, Penelope was put in the center of the front row (just like every other year).

Honestly, Penelope had no idea why she had ever thought that she and Rita could get along. Rita hadn't just been mean since birth. She had probably been mean when she was in her mother's tummy, or even *before* that.

If there was a competition for meanest girl, Rita would win it hands-down.

Penelope realized her hands were on her

hips. She wasn't sure when she'd put them there. Her palms felt sweaty. Her temples throbbed and her cheeks felt hot. Really hot.

"YOU MIGHT BE OLDER. AND YOU MIGHT BE TALLER," she yelled. "BUT YOU'RE NOT THE ONE WHO HAS HER BOOKS IN ALPHABETICAL ORDER IN HER LOCKER. YOU'RE NOT THE ONE WHO HAS A REPUTATION FOR BEING ORGANIZED AT ALL TIMES. YOU ONLY HAVE A REPUTATION FOR BEING MEAN AT ALL TIMES. YOU WOULD BE THE WORST LEADER IN HISTORY."

"You're such a baby, Penelope Kingston," Rita said. "You need to calm. Right. Down. Seriously! You look like a freak, your face is so red. Look, you've even got veins popping out of your temples. Gross."

Even though there were tears pricking at her eyes, Penelope did not cry. But she had already done the very worst thing. She had broken rule number one—her most important rule.

Penelope gulped. She pressed her fingers to her temples, trying to flatten out the veins, and reminded herself to breathe.

Looking around, she could see that Bob had moved over to stand near the door. Tilly was right next to her. This seemed unsupportive of a very best friend, even if the bell *was* ringing for the next activity.

Even though it was painful to talk, Penelope forced herself to calm down. It was absolutely essential to get both of their votes. She took a deep breath and squeezed out the words, "Bob and Tilly, who do you think should be cabin leader?"

Bob and Tilly stepped farther away to talk privately.

As they waited for a response, Penelope and Rita stared at each other. Penelope tried to look directly into Rita's eyes, but they were very intense, so after a while she switched to her mouth. Then her ears.

Finally, Bob and Tilly came back.

"We think we probably don't need a leader at all . . . ," Bob began.

"But if you guys are so keen on having one . . . ," Tilly continued.

"Then maybe it should be both of you," Bob finished.

Then, without waiting for a response, they turned and ran out of the cabin.

Penelope was very rarely late for anything, but this time she ignored the bell and stayed in the cabin all by herself. Outbursts were exhausting, and this had been quite a big one. She just wanted to curl up in her bunk bed and make it all go away.

She wasn't even sure which part she was *most* upset about. But Bob being so unsupportive was definitely one part. If Penelope had one wish right then, she would wish for Bob to come back and apologize to her. Unfortunately (and Penelope tried it, just in case), her wish didn't work.

Of course, the other thing that was truly upsetting was that she had already (on the very first day!) broken her number one rule. Penelope reached over to her bag and pulled the list out of its secret pocket. She would have to make some changes. But she was sure she would feel better when she was done.

Penelope hunted through the drawers at

the bottom of the wardrobe in the corner. One drawer was empty, but in the other one, Penelope found blank paper, double-sided tape, and three sharpened pencils. Even though the pencil didn't match the pen she'd used to write her list, Penelope was able to make the alteration quite neatly.

Just as she was finishing, Ramon poked his head around the door. "There you are, Penelope," he said. "They're waiting for you at bike ed. Come along with me."

Penelope quickly put her list in the drawer so that Ramon wouldn't see it, then closed the drawer and followed him.

Penelope steered her bike through the crossover in the figure eight that was painted on the basketball court. After only a slight wobble, she was off again.

It was her third time riding around the course. Each time, she had found it a little bit easier. Each time, she felt more confident.

She had passed Rita twice as they made their way around the course. Penelope had been concentrating very hard on trying to make up for being six minutes late by doing everything right. But Rita had a great big smile plastered on her face. Penelope wondered if the smile was pretend. *She* certainly didn't feel like smiling.

"Great stuff," the bike ed teacher called out. "Now we're going to try riding two abreast, straight up to the line and back again. Steer the bike with your outside hand, and hang on to your partner's hand on the inside. Then we'll come back the other way."

Penelope looked to her right. Her partner was Bob.

Bob's bike helmet covered all of her very short hair.

WHEN SHE SMILED A SMALL (GUILTY?) GRIN AT PENELOPE, SHE LOOKED LIKE AN EGG WITH TEETH.

Penelope felt a surge of disappointment. She couldn't believe that Bob hadn't stuck up for her. That disappointment brought a wave of loneliness.

It was a type of loneliness Penelope had experienced many times before. But that was before she had a very best friend.

"Are you okay, Pen?" Bob whispered, and

she took Penelope's hand. "Let's talk after this. Just the two of us?"

Penelope nodded. She was relieved that Bob wanted to talk. Perhaps her friend *was* going to apologize? Even if it was a little bit late, Penelope would definitely accept Bob's apology as graciously as she could.

SHE WAS SURPRISED TO FIND THAT SHE WAS ABLE TO RIDE WITH ONE HAND WHILE HOLDING BOB'S HAND WITH THE OTHER.

IF THEY GOT TOO FAR APART, WHICH HAPPENED A FEW TIMES, THEY WOULD JUST LET GO UNTIL THEY COULD GET CLOSER AGAIN.

THEN THEY WOULD HOLD HANDS A LITTLE MORE TIGHTLY.

It felt like an excellent (and timely) reminder about how to steer a (very) best friendship.

CHAPTER

Penelope and Bob were sitting on a bench seat in the laundry room. They'd chosen it for privacy. All around them spun dryers filled with linen, filling the air with a low, warm hum.

Penelope waited for Bob to speak. In fact, she waited quite a while. In the end she decided to start.

"I forgive you," Penelope said.

Bob looked at her and shook her head. "Geez, Pen," was all she said.

Penelope frowned. Perhaps she needed to explain more. "Obviously, since you're my very best friend, I expected you to stick up for me when Rita was being so mean. And I expected you to vote for me to be cabin leader."

"Pen, you *know* Rita can be mean. But what you said, and how you said it . . ." Bob made a motion with her hands. It looked like a rocket taking off into the sky. "You actually told her that everyone thinks she's mean. And that she would be the worst leader in history. That was pretty mean, too, when you think about it."

Sometimes, Penelope could not remember everything she said during an outburst. Being reminded that she'd said Rita would be the worst leader in history gave her a bit of a head-ache. And the fact that Bob thought Penelope had been mean was upsetting. She rubbed her forehead.

"I tried not to react, Bob. I really did."

"Rita will always try to make you go crazy, Pen. You can't let her drive you nutso."

Penelope did not like the use of the word "nutso." Still, Bob had a point.

"You know, Tilly and I couldn't care less whether you're the leader or Rita's the leader or there's no leader at all," Bob continued. "Look, we don't even really care if we win the competition. Not if it's going to make everyone all grumpy and sad. What we *do* care about is having fun at camp."

Penelope scratched her head. It was very difficult to believe that Bob and Tilly didn't care about winning the best cabin competition. She actually understood Rita's point of view better—Rita obviously cared about the competition as much as Penelope did. But one thing Penelope loved about Bob was that she never *pretended* to feel something she didn't actually feel.

Maybe that was more important than having a best friend who would vote for her no matter what. Even if it gave Penelope a headache.

"I can be fun sometimes, can't I?" she asked.

Bob nodded energetically.

"The BEST fun," she declared. "*Nutso* fun!"

Penelope stood up and held out her hand. When Bob took it, Penelope yanked her upright. Then she gave Bob a (friendly) punch in the arm.

"Let's go and have some fun," she said.

It was just as well that Penelope and Bob found themselves sitting with Joanna and Eliza at dinner. If they'd had to sit with Rita, Penelope was not entirely sure what she would do. Ever since Bob had pointed out that she had been quite mean herself, Penelope felt a bit funny about seeing Rita again.

"Maybe the best thing is to ignore Rita. She can do her own thing while we get on with making cabin seven awesome," Penelope suggested to Bob.

Although Penelope strongly believed that best cabin competition tactics should be kept private, she didn't bother whispering. The dining hall was very noisy. Across the table, Joanna was picking up peas from her plate and very sneakily (so the teachers couldn't see) tossing them over to where the boys were sitting. It was very distracting, but Penelope tried to focus.

"I was thinking we could position our spare shoes in the shape of a heart outside the door.

And clean up and stack all the bags in a creative way. I also think it would be quite unique to label the recycling bin—"

But before Penelope could finish her sentence, a glob of mashed potato flew neatly through the air and splattered on her cheek in a totally unacceptable way. Admittedly, Penelope could not imagine a glob of mashed potato splattering on her cheek in a way that *was* acceptable.

Before she could get too mad, though, Alex was right beside her.

"I am so, so sorry, Penelope," he said, so sincerely that Penelope had to assume it was either a freak accident or that Alex was having another very odd moment.

"That's okay, I guess, Alex," Penelope said, wiping her cheek with a napkin.

But before Penelope could say another

word, Alex was across the other side of the table *rubbing a glob of mashed potato into Joanna's hair.*

Joanna was just sitting there, letting it happen. Penelope decided Joanna must be in shock. Bits of mashed potato fell from her hair, covering the table in a kind of mini-avalanche.

Then Joanna proceeded to have a fit. Of *laughter.* If she didn't know better, Penelope would even say that Joanna looked delighted.

Penelope was astonished. Why would having mashed potato rubbed into your hair be something to laugh about?

Her face must have shown her puzzlement, because Bob leaned in and cupped Penelope's ear, whispering, "They're crushing on each other so bad."

Aha! Penelope thought about Alex showing off at the challenge swing, and sticking

Florence up his shirt and bumping into Joanna. Now that Bob had pointed it out, her explanation did seem possible. But if *crushing* involved such strange and unusual behavior, Penelope hoped it would NEVER happen to her.

Still, she was grateful that Bob had shared this information. She would never have been able to figure it out without a very best friend to help her.

Penelope was also extremely glad that she'd had that talk with Bob. Having a very best friend with totally different opinions could be a bit puzzling sometimes. And, clearly, Bob sometimes understood things that Penelope didn't. But Penelope was beginning to think this was a GOOD thing. Even though it made Penelope see things in a way that sometimes gave her headaches, it was also pretty important.

So when Bob told her she wanted to do outdoor cooking after dinner instead of coming to art with Penelope, Penelope didn't make a big deal about it. In fact, she thought she was quite gracious about it.

Penelope stifled a yawn as she walked back to the cabin with Tilly after art.

"Wow," Tilly said, pausing to look up at the night sky.

"Wow," Penelope echoed, stopping beside her.

The crescent moon hung above them, brighter and bigger than it ever looked in the city, and there seemed to be more stars in the sky than Penelope had ever seen before. It was a bit like the glow-in-the-dark planetarium ceiling in Grandpa George's living room, but even more majestic.

"It makes you feel small, doesn't it?" Tilly

said. She nudged Penelope and giggled. "No offense. I mean for all of us, not just you."

Penelope smiled. "No offense taken," she said. She breathed in the fresh night air. "It makes me feel like there are so many possibilities."

Tilly nodded. "As though we're a tiny jigsaw piece in something huge and special," she added.

The girls gazed upward in silence. The funny thing was, it was not an awkward silence at all. Penelope hadn't had much one-on-one time with Tilly before. She hadn't known that Tilly was so good at drawing until tonight, and she hadn't known that Tilly thought the same sort of deep thoughts that sometimes ran around in Penelope's own head.

In a way, it had been good that Bob and Rita had chosen to do outdoor cooking, rather than art. In fact, it was quite lovely to find another friend who enjoyed art as much as she did. Penelope and Tilly had drawn six very lovely pictures between them. There was only one blank wall in the cabin (because of the bunks and the doors), but Penelope was already visualizing some excellent ways to arrange their artwork. Plus, spending some time with just Tilly had been nice. Penelope was now quite sure that Tilly wasn't the type of girl who would steal someone's very best friend.

Just then they heard a sound.

"Woooo."

The girls looked at each other. Penelope smiled and nudged Tilly (she thought about pinching her, but decided it might be a bit early in their friendship). Even if she didn't know Bob's voice inside out and back to front, the shadow that was cast on the wall of the laundry room was unmistakable.

"OH NO, TILLY," PENELOPE SAID LOUDLY. "IS THAT A GHOST?"

Tilly covered her mouth so she wouldn't laugh out loud. "Maybe," she said, pausing. Then, "I think it's the scariest kind of ghost. A Bob-shaped ghost!"

"Okay, you got me," Bob squealed, falling into step beside them.

She had a loaf of charcoal-colored bread, which she offered to Penelope and Tilly. They each tore off a bit.

"It's not bad," Tilly said, "if you like things burnt to a cinder."

"Mmm, crunchy," Penelope added. Perhaps it was because she was overtired, but everything was making her giggly. And those giggles were infectious.

When they arrived back at cabin seven, though, they stopped giggling.

The porch light was switched on. Two rows

of their shoes, set in the same pattern either side, created a walkway from the steps to the door. Rita had stuck red cardboard along the wooden floorboards. The effect was something like a homemade red carpet.

"That looks so cool!" Tilly exclaimed.

She and Bob started to pretend they were movie stars, waving and blowing kisses at their imaginary audience.

Penelope agreed that the entrance looked good. Maybe even better than her shoe heart would have looked. But she was wary.

"I thought Rita did outdoor cooking with you," Penelope whispered to Bob.

"She did," Bob replied. "But she said she was tired and came back early."

Now Penelope was even MORE wary. She followed the girls inside.

Rita *did* look tired, but she had obviously not been resting.

"So, fellow cabin sevensies," said Rita, "what do you think?"

While the others told Rita how good the cabin looked, Penelope made her own inspection. She could hardly believe how neat it was. All their bags and backpacks were stacked in order of size. The four camp booklets stood upright, fanned open in a neat row on the bench.

When Penelope saw that Rita had made labels for the recycling bin and the trash bin, and stuck them on with tape, she was quite impressed.

But then she noticed that the drawer under the wardrobe was open, and empty. And that there was something stuck to the wall with tape.

LIST FOR CAMP SUCCESS

1.   No outbursts
     (unless people are ABSOLUTELY mean)

2.   No crying

3.   Win (at least one) prize

4.   Try most activities ? ***

"Ta-da!" Rita said, pointing at Penelope's list. She was laughing. "I found it in the drawer." She turned to Bob and Tilly. "Can you even believe it? Isn't it *hysterical*?"

Penelope felt as though her heart had dropped out of her chest and landed in her tummy. It was possibly the most humiliating moment of her entire life.

"That's private, Rita," Penelope said, her voice wobbling. "It's My PRIVATE List."

Penelope felt Bob move closer and put her arm around her.

"I know!" Rita giggled. "That's what makes it so funny. It's such a babyish thing to do. '*Unless people are ABSOLUTELY mean,*'" she said in a mimicking way. "And I think I know all about rule number four, Penelope. You're totally planning to chicken out of the challenge swing."

Penelope felt all the familiar beginnings of an outburst. The pulsing in her temples, the heat in her face. THE ANGRY WORDS BUBBLING INSIDE HER, GETTING READY TO LEAP OUT OF HER MOUTH.

But something stopped her. Perhaps it was seeing the list there, with the words "No outbursts" right in front of her. Or maybe it was Bob's arm around her shoulders, and remembering Bob's earlier comments. Bob was right. She couldn't let Rita drive her nutso.

WHATEVER IT WAS, IT LASTED LONG ENOUGH FOR THE WAVE OF ANGER PENELOPE WAS FEELING TO PASS.

Just then, Tilly did something totally unexpected. As the other three watched, she went over to the wall and peeled the list off. She handed it to Penelope.

"You shouldn't do things like that, Rita," Tilly said. Her voice was a little bit wobbly. Tilly had never criticized Rita before. It was very brave of her, and it definitely made Penelope feel a little bit better.

"Yeah, you really need to lay off Penelope, Rita," Bob added.

Rita rolled her eyes as though the whole thing was no big deal, but Penelope could tell that she was quite shocked. Her eyebrows were knitted together, and she mumbled something about being the only normal one in the cabin.

Then Rita looked at the clock, which was now the only thing decorating the cabin wall. "It's lights-out time," she said. "No talking. That's a RULE."

It was eight minutes past midnight. Penelope was very tired, but she couldn't stop thinking about everything that had happened on her first day at camp.

Bob's snoring wasn't helping, either. Honestly, it had taken Bob about thirty seconds to fall asleep. After tossing and turning in her sleeping bag for a while, Tilly seemed to have gone to sleep, too.

Penelope thought that Rita had also drifted off. But then Penelope heard her talking.

"No. Don't."

For a moment, Penelope thought she might be going to say something about putting her Private List on the wall. But there was something hazy about Rita's voice that stopped Penelope from responding.

"Not. Baby. Nooo. Janine, nooo."

This time, Rita's words came out as kind of a moan, and Penelope understood what was happening. Rita was sleep-talking. She must have been having a dream. And whatever she was dreaming about didn't sound very pleasant.

Penelope thought she heard a little sob before Rita's breathing became even again.

Penelope could have done without Rita

being in her cabin. She could have done without Rita being in her whole life, actually. But she didn't like to hear anyone being upset. Even if it *was* just a dream. She rolled over and tried to put it out of her mind. Dreams didn't necessarily have anything to do with real life.

Besides, the last thing she needed was to waste time feeling sorry for Rita Azul! She had a huge day looming ahead of her. The challenge swing was scheduled for eleven a.m.

Penelope liked things to be Clear and Definite, but there was nothing Clear or Definite about what was going to happen at eleven a.m. Penelope still had no idea how she was going to handle the situation.

No. Idea. At. All.

CHAPTER

Breakfast was strangely quiet. There were no food fights, and everyone seemed to be eating less than they had the day before. After breakfast, they all went on a beach walk. It was a lovely day, so perhaps they were just soaking that in. But Penelope had her doubts.

One thing was certain. Her own tummy was flipping. Over and over again.

On the way to the challenge swing, the tummy flipping got worse. Penelope was glad she had her very best friend right beside her. Near the front, Alex had started a wave, which rippled back toward Penelope and Bob. When it reached them, Penelope found that she couldn't throw up her hands properly.

"You know what, Pen?" Bob said, turning toward her. "You look really pale. You don't have to do it if you don't want to. Don't worry about what anyone else thinks."

Penelope breathed deeply.

"But *you're* going to do it, right?" she asked Bob.

Bob nodded. "Yeah. I'm pumped to try it," she said (in her usual honest way, not in a pretending way). "But look. Plenty of kids are freaking out. Look at Felix Unger."

Penelope looked ahead. Felix Unger (who was actually excellent at most sports) was sneaking backward. In fact, he sneaked right past them, moving to the very back of the line. This seemed like a fairly good clue that Felix was feeling nervous. It also seemed to Penelope like a Very Good Idea.

In fact, now that she was looking around, Penelope could see other kids were clearly feeling nervous, too. Alison Cromwell turning around and going cross-eyed, then laughing in a crazy way, was another hint. Knowing she wasn't the only one who felt anxious made Penelope feel a tiny bit better.

Alex Gabriel went first. Penelope helped pull the rope with the others, but her arms felt extremely weak and the shouts of encouragement from the other kids were just background noise. All she could think about was how nervous she was.

Penelope watched as Alex rose into the sky, higher and higher, until he was as high as

the swing could possibly go. He didn't hesi-
tate before pulling the release handle. As he
plummeted toward the ground he stretched
his right arm out like Superman, just like he
had said he would. He really did look like he
was swooping down to rescue someone. But
when he got off the swing he was just plain
old show-off Alex, trying to get everyone in
the line to high-five him.

Joanna was next up. "Oh my gosh," she
squealed, after Ramon had secured the harness
and told her she was good to go. "This thing's
giving me a massive wedgie!"

Loads of kids laughed. Penelope tried to
smile, but it was a difficult thing to do when
she felt so drained and weak. Oscar Finley must
have noticed, because right after Joanna had
her turn, he dropped out from his spot near the
front of the line and came over to her.

"Are you okay, Penny?" he asked. "You look kind of weird."

Penelope shook her head. Perhaps she should be pretending she was okay, but somehow she couldn't find it in her.

"Hey, Bob, do you mind if I take Penny back in the line a bit?" he asked.

"Nope. Good idea, Oscar," Bob said kindly.

With each step away from the challenge swing, Penelope felt a little better. Soon they reached the back of the line.

"You don't need to be nervous," Oscar said. "Just go as high as you want. I've been on one of these before. You get a jolt and it's scary for a second. Then it's just really good fun. You'll be fine."

Penelope grimaced, but she also felt a bit less shaky. One thing she knew about Oscar Finley was that he was *not* a liar.

"Also," Oscar said, leaning forward with a very serious expression, "heaps of kids have done this before you, and no one has died."

Penelope felt a genuine smile playing on her lips. "Well, I didn't actually expect to die," she said.

"Good," Oscar said, grinning now, "because you're *probably* not going to."

Oscar stayed with Penelope right up until his turn. It was kind of funny how kids kept chickening out and coming to the back of the line. By the time it was Penelope's turn, there were six people behind her. One of them was Rita Azul. Penelope supposed that she wanted to go last so everyone was paying attention when she sang her terrible song, and not worrying about their own turn.

Then it was Penelope's turn. When Ramon fastened her harness, Penelope had to remind herself to breathe. She clung tightly to the rope as she rose through the air. The green handle was right there beside her. About halfway up, she thought about telling the others to stop. She thought about it again three-quarters of the way up. But somehow, she kept going up and up, and it was kind of okay.

From the HIGHEST point of the challenge swing (sixty feet!—but this wasn't the time to think about that) Penelope could see the whole camp. The ocean glittered as though it was made of diamonds. Penelope was filled with fear.

But she also felt something bigger than fear. A kind of exhilaration that she'd never felt before.

"Okay, Penelope. Pull the handle on three," Ramon called out. "One!"

There was still time to back out. Penelope could ask Ramon and the other kids to lower her down.

"Two!"

Or she could go halfway down, and do it from there.

"Three!"

Or she could do it. Right now.

Penelope pulled the handle. There was a jolt as she dropped. Her heart lurched into her gut.

PENELOPE FELT LIKE A BIRD. SHE FELT LIKE A JET PLANE. SHE FELT SERIOUSLY ALIVE!

Then Penelope PLUMMETED to the ground.

It was over in seconds, but those seconds on the swing felt longer than normal seconds.

She was still giddy and excited when her feet touched the ground.

"You were amazing!" Bob cried, helping Ramon unfasten the harness. "Totes fearless."

Penelope's breaths came quickly. "I actually did it!" she squealed. "I DID IT!" Her legs were shaky as she got out of the harness and walked beside her very best friend.

"It's cool, right?" Bob said. "I loved it." Bob gave Penelope one of her cheekiest looks. "Should we beg Ramon to let us do it again?"

Penelope giggled as she shook her head. There was absolutely NO WAY she was doing it again. But she felt extremely proud. She'd discovered a new part of herself.

A part of herself that was brave enough

to do something that terrified her. A part she'd never even known existed.

It was actually fun to help with the ropes. Penelope felt strong, knowing her turn was over and done with. Felix Unger called stop almost as soon as he started rising. He said it was because of a painful wedgie, but Penelope suspected that wasn't the real reason.

Tilly went halfway and squealed with delight all the way down. Eliza and Alison both screamed their heads off, but still wanted to go right back and do it again.

Rita Azul was last. As Ramon was about to strap her into the harness, Penelope braced herself to hear that awful song.

But then something very strange happened. Rita shook her head wildly. Then, without a single word, she turned and ran off.

☆ ☆ ☆

"She's not in the cabin," Tilly said. "We've looked everywhere!"

Penelope bit her lip. She didn't need to be an excellent detective to know something was wrong.

Penelope thought about Rita moaning in her sleep. Perhaps her bad dream had something to do with all this? If Rita was feeling upset, it made sense that she'd go somewhere comforting. . . .

"I think I know where she is," Penelope said suddenly, breaking away from the group.

Penelope stood in the doorway of the barn. Rita was facing away from Penelope. She had Florence on her lap, and was stroking the guinea pig's extra-long fur. It was clear she was pouring her heart out.

"I'm such a baby. But it was too high . . . so

scary. I'll have to lie about it to Janine. . . ."

Penelope didn't know who Janine was, but she recognized the name from Rita's sleep-talking last night.

Florence made a noise that sounded like a cross between a squeaky toy and a cooing pigeon. Rita lifted the guinea pig up to her chest for a cuddle.

"Maybe I *am* a baby," she said, and the sad way she said it wound its way into Penelope's heart. There was nothing nice about seeing Rita like this, even if she was terribly mean some-times. Penelope walked in and sat beside Rita.

"You're not a baby, Rita," Penelope said softly. "The challenge swing *is* crazy high. It makes a lot of sense to be afraid. I was."

Rita looked at Penelope. There were tears in her eyes. "But even *you* did it," she said (which wasn't the nicest thing to say, but Penelope forgave her).

"Well, I had help," she said. "Oscar gave me a pep talk. He was great."

Rita drew in a breath. "It's not just the challenge swing," she said. "It's *everything*."

Penelope tilted her head to the side. She wanted to help. But "everything" covered an awful lot of things. She wasn't sure where to start.

"Who's Janine?" she asked.

The tears spilled over and started flowing down Rita's cheeks. Penelope thought about rubbing her back (that's what people always did on TV), but she wasn't so sure that would be the right thing to do, so she kept her hands by her sides.

"My big sister," Rita said. "She's going to give me such a hard time if I don't do the challenge swing." Rita wiped her tears away with the back of her hand. Florence squeak-cooed again. "We used to be really close. But Janine started high school this year and she's totally changed. She won't sit next to me on the bus and she keeps going on about me being a baby. She's really, really mean."

Penelope thought of all the times that Rita had been really, really mean. There was no doubt she'd been even meaner this year. Penelope thought that might have something to do with her sister, but decided not to mention it.

"My brother, Harry, got a bit strange when he started high school," Penelope offered.

Rita looked interested, so Penelope continued. "For the first two weeks, he wouldn't walk me to the school gates if any of his friends were watching. He said it was embarrassing."

Rita sniffed. "Janine won't walk with me at all," she said. "I have to stay twenty paces behind her. She says I stink."

Ouch. Harry had never been quite *that* mean.

Rita did not smell. Penelope had a sneaking suspicion that *extreme* meanness might run in Rita's family.

"But you know," Penelope said, "once Harry got used to high school things kind of went back to normal." She paused to think about what she was saying. "Or maybe we just made a new normal. I'm not sure it was ever exactly the same again, but it was okay."

Rita sighed. "I don't want a new normal," she whispered. "I just want the old normal back."

Penelope didn't quite know what to say to that. She was pretty sure that old normals never came back. But instead of saying that, she just sat next to Rita and watched her pet Florence.

"If we *have* to find a new normal," said Rita, "do you think Janine and I might get one that's good?"

Penelope breathed deeply. She thought about

how very strange and awful it had been when her dad had first left them to make a new family. It had definitely felt like things would never be normal again, let alone good. Yet somehow, over time, she and Harry and even her mom had become used to it.

Now it really was okay to see him some weekends and on the school holidays rather than every night. Perhaps it wasn't a *perfect* normal, but it was definitely okay most of the time.

"I do," Penelope said. "Absolutely."

It was very pleasing to see a smile creeping onto Rita's face, even if it was just a small one.

"I'm sorry I put your list up like that, Penelope," Rita said. "You know, I make lists, too. I've got loads of them at home. I'll show you sometime."

Penelope bit her lip. It was nice of Rita to admit she made lists, too, but Penelope didn't think she wanted to go to Rita's house. It probably wasn't the right time to tell her that, though. Despite all the horrid things Rita had said and done, this was the very first time that she had ever apologized to Penelope. It was quite a shock. But it was a good shock.

"I'm sorry, too," Penelope said. "I shouldn't have said you'd be the worst leader in history. You made the cabin look amazing. I don't think I could have done much better myself."

"Neither do I," Rita replied, but the way she said it was more funny than mean.

Penelope decided to smile.

"What do *you* think, Florence?" Rita asked, lifting Florence up. Penelope reached out and petted her long, soft fur.

Just then, Penelope noticed something. She giggled. "Florence thinks she might make a better listener if you talk to her face rather than her bottom."

Both girls were still laughing when Rita got up and put Florence back in her enclosure.

"Come on, Penelope," she said, holding out her hand. "I want to see if there's still time to have a go at the challenge swing. If you'll be my support person."

THERE WAS ABSOLUTELY NOTHING SMALL ABOUT RITA'S LAUGH AS SHE TURNED THE POOR GUINEA PIG UP THE OTHER WAY.

CHAPTER

9

In the afternoon, Penelope's cabin joined other cabin groups for orienteering. Bob and Tilly weren't much help finding Bats' Belfry (which was halfway up the trunk of a very big tree), but Rita was extremely cooperative and (mostly) very good with a compass. Penelope's group was the first to find Vampire Alley and check it off their list. Unfortunately, there were a few problems finding Horror Highway (as in, going south instead of north for a good fifteen minutes before Penelope realized Rita's mistake). By the time they got to Coffin Curves, three cabin groups were already there. But after doing the challenge swing that morning (and going all the way to the Very Top!), Penelope didn't feel so bad.

After all, she was pretty sure they had an **EXCELLENT** chance of winning the best cabin competition. Right after orienteering, the girls had decorated the wall with Penelope and Tilly's drawings. Penelope thought they looked amazing.

Dinner had been spaghetti and meatballs, which was just about everyone's favorite meal in the world. After that, everyone had played charades.

Now the girls were tucked into their bunks. The atmosphere in cabin seven on the second (and very last) night of camp was totally different to the first night. *Everybody* was happy.

Even though it was past lights-out time, and they were supposed to be quietly falling asleep, every single girl in cabin seven had broken that rule at least twice. Penelope knew it was (a bit) wrong to keep talking, but the happy feelings inside her were wriggling about like crazy. In fact, they were wriggling about so much that a very *unusual* and very **NOT-PENELOPE** suggestion popped right out of her mouth.

"Pillow fight, anyone?" she suggested.

She climbed down, leaned over the top bunk, and swung her pillow into Bob's leg— and then into Tilly's arm, and finally hit Rita (just a little bit harder) on her right ear.

Everyone was silent for a split second, as

though they were extremely surprised. Then the silence turned into squeals and thwacks as they belted each other with pillows (which was *probably* quite safe).

AND THANKS TO PENELOPE KINGSTON, THE GIGGLES COMING FROM CABIN SEVEN CONTINUED WELL AFTER LIGHTS-OUT.

The next morning after breakfast, all the kids gathered in the main hall. It was hard to believe they would be leaving Camp Tribute in less than an hour. In some ways, the time had flown. But somehow it also felt like it had been longer than forty-eight hours. So many things had happened.

Penelope remembered Rachel's first words to them: *You will take from this camp whatever you put into it.*

Now Rachel was handing out awards. She was about to announce the winner of the best cabin competition. Next to Penelope, Bob and Tilly were comparing something in their Camp Tribute booklets and not paying attention to the announcement. Penelope leaned forward, looking past Bob and Tilly.

She reached over and tapped Rita on the knee. "Good luck," she whispered.

Rita screwed up her nose and bit her lip, looking as nervous as Penelope. Then she showed Penelope her crossed fingers. Instantly, Penelope crossed her own on both hands.

As much as she'd loved camp, she was looking forward to going home and seeing her mom and her brother (who was not mean very often), and Grandpa George. It would be amazing to go home with a best cabin medal to make them all proud. If her cabin won, Penelope would definitely wear her medal on the bus ride home, and would strongly suggest that Bob, Tilly, and Rita do the same. After that, it could live on her jewelry stand. Or perhaps she could hang it on the wall with her award certificates. There were many options to consider.

"The winner of this year's best cabin competition is . . ."

Penelope waited as Oscar Finley and Tommy Stratton did a drumroll on the floorboards. She looked over at Rita. They each held their crossed fingers in front of their faces.

". . . Cabin six!" Rachel announced with a flourish. "Joanna, Eliza, Alison, and Sarah."

Right away, Alex jumped up and yelled, "Go, Jo!" three times very loudly, while pumping his hand in the air. Then he ran over to Joanna and punched her on the arm.

It was a very strange sight, and for a moment, Penelope forgot to be disappointed about not winning.

But she definitely felt a pang of jealousy when she saw the girls hold up their medals. Bob squeezed Penelope's knee. Penelope glanced over at Rita. She was frowning, and her mouth was a downward slash. Penelope waited for her own jealous pang to grow into bitter disappointment or anger. She definitely felt deflated.

But somehow, she just didn't feel all that

terrible. The best cabin competition and the lovely medals didn't seem quite so important anymore. It was actually nice to see Joanna (who normally only got attention for being naughty) win a prize.

Before Penelope had time to be properly surprised at how fine she was, Rachel had moved on.

"And now, this is my personal favorite," Rachel said. "The prize for the best support person. This is for someone who has tried very hard themselves, but has still found the energy and goodwill to support others."

The award Rachel held up was not as flashy as the best cabin medals. In fact, it was just a piece of paper. A certificate. The Old Penelope, the Penelope who hadn't been to Camp Tribute, would not have admired it very much. But

New Penelope thought it looked pretty special. She hoped Oscar Finley would win it. She'd nominated him, but the final judgments were left to the camp leaders.

Penelope looked across the hall. It was very good timing, because right at that moment, Oscar Finley happened to be looking right back at her. Just as he'd done at the very beginning of camp, he gave Penelope another of his big, generous overhead waves. For a moment, Penelope considered responding with a small wave again, so no one could see. But then she reconsidered. After all, a wave was just something you did with a friend. It wasn't silly like yelling out or punching arms or getting into headlocks or letting someone rub globs of mashed potato in your hair. And it certainly didn't mean you were crushing.

If kids wanted to be silly about her and Oscar waving to each other, then she would just ignore them.

Penelope lifted her arm up above her head and waved.

FROM ACROSS THE HALL, PENELOPE COULD SEE OSCAR'S BEAMING SMILE.

"And the winner is . . ." Rachel paused, drawing out the moment. ". . . Penelope Kingston!"

Penelope walked up the steps of the bus and turned to take one last look at Camp Tribute. Suddenly, she had a flash of understanding about the text her grandpa had sent her the night before camp.

> Enjoy the ride. Remember the journey is just as important as the destination.

It actually made sense. In fact, it made a LOT of sense.

She plopped happily into the seat next to Bob, and smiled to herself. Grandpa hadn't been talking about the bus trip. The journey wasn't just the journey to school camp. It was the whole experience of going to camp. It wasn't just the good things, either. It was also the not-so-good things, because they were all part of the experience.